An Artist's

PENCILS

F. Isabel Campoy
Alma Flor Ada

ALFAGUARA
YOUNG READERS
SANTILLANA

Originally published in Spanish as *Lápices*

Art Director: Felipe Dávalos
Design: Arroyo+Cerda S.C.
Editor: Norman Duarte

Cover: Frida Kahlo, *Self-Portrait,* 1930

Santillana USA Publishing Company, Inc.
2105 NW 86th Avenue
Miami, FL 33122

Art D: *Pencils*

ISBN: 1-58105-589-7

Printed in Colombia.
D'Vinni Editorial Ltda.

Contents

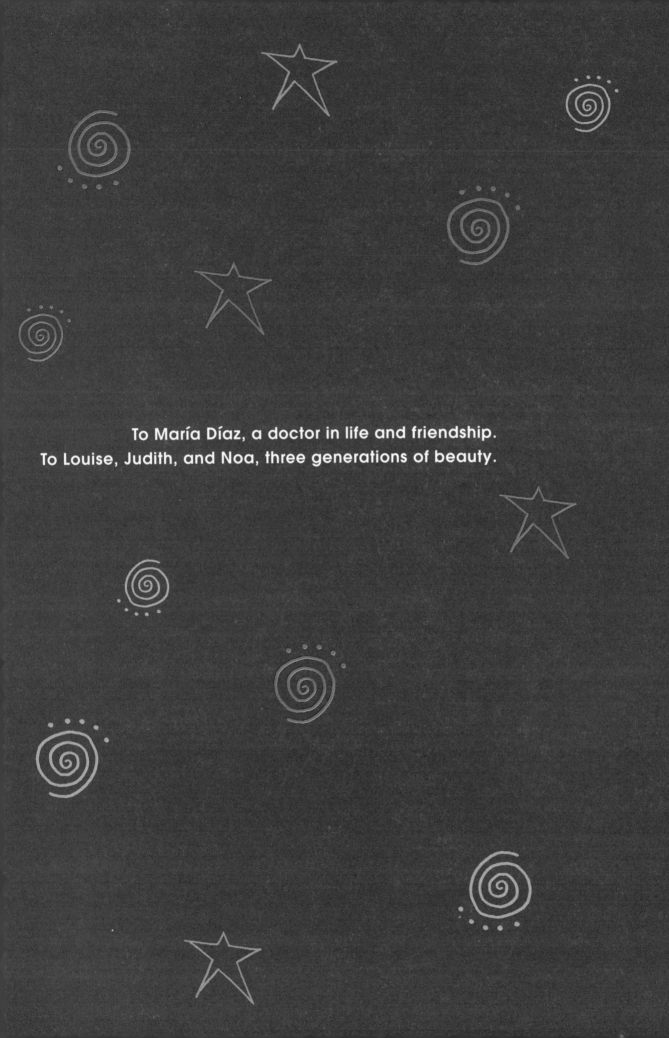

To María Díaz, a doctor in life and friendship.
To Louise, Judith, and Noa, three generations of beauty.

I spy

In this painting, Diego Rivera painted many important figures from the artistic and social worlds.

Here we see José Martí, Diego Rivera himself, his wife Frida Kahlo, José Guadalupe Posada, and General Porfirio Díaz, among others.

❖ **D**escribe five things that are going on in this painting.

Dream of a Sunday Afternoon in the Alameda
Diego Rivera

✣ Simón Silva ✣

Simón Silva was born in Calexico, California, to a family of farm workers. He grew up among golden and red mornings, sun, and earth.
And that is what you see in his paintings and his book illustrations.
Simón is a well-known artist. With love and respect, he paints scenes of life in the fields. His first book was *Gathering the Sun*, Alma Flor Ada's book of poems written to honor farm workers.

He has also illustrated *The Butterfly*, a book of childhood memories by a university professor, also the son of farm workers, Francisco Jiménez.

✤ **J**ust as Simón paints what he sees around him, adding what he feels, you can also paint something you see every day and you like.

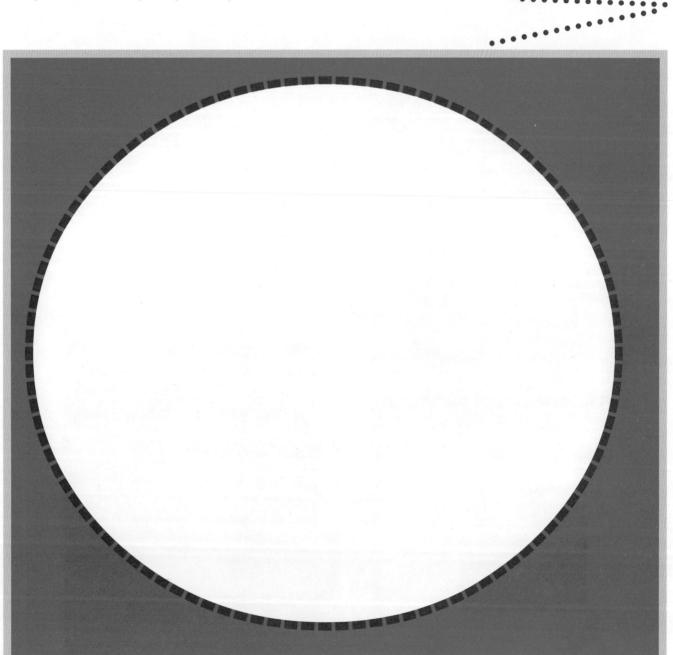

Your drawing

Self-portrait

✢ **A** self-portrait is a painting in which the artist paints her or himself.

✢ **L**ook at these self-portraits.

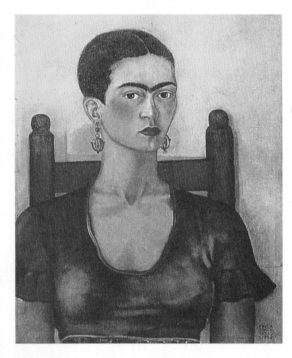

Self-portrait
Frida Kahlo

Self-portrait
Francisco de Goya

Do your own self-portrait

❖ **L**ooking at yourself in a mirror, focus on the things
that are most characteristic of you: your hair, the color of your eyes…

❖ **P**erhaps you would like to add some object that you like,
like a book or a toy, to your portrait…

❖ **T**his is a piece of art for your private collection.

Ceramics

✛ **C**eramic jars and vases are usually round and are made from a little clay that is shaped with the hands as a round table spins.

✛ **T**his potter gives shape to a jar in Albacete, Spain.

✛ **Y**ou can also be a potter. With some clay, make your own piece.

Pottery in Albacete, Spain

Hand in hand with...

❖ Héctor Viveros Lee ❖

Héctor Viveros Lee is a young Hispanic artist who lives in San Francisco, California.

Héctor is also a bilingual teacher and knows children well.

He likes to paint animals and to play with words in his two languages, Spanish and English.

Héctor knows how to look at color and re-create it beautifully with his pencils on paper. His characters are full of tenderness.

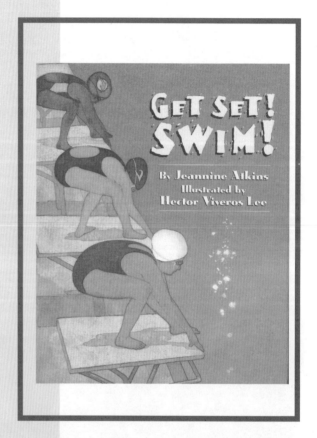

❖ **O**n a separate piece of paper, draw a picture of an animal you like. Fill the entire page with color.

Museums

✢ Art museums are filled with the masterpieces
of famous artists.

The paintings in public museums belong to everybody,
and they are there for everybody to admire.

In the Hispanic world there are many important museums.
One of them is the Prado Museum in Madrid, Spain.

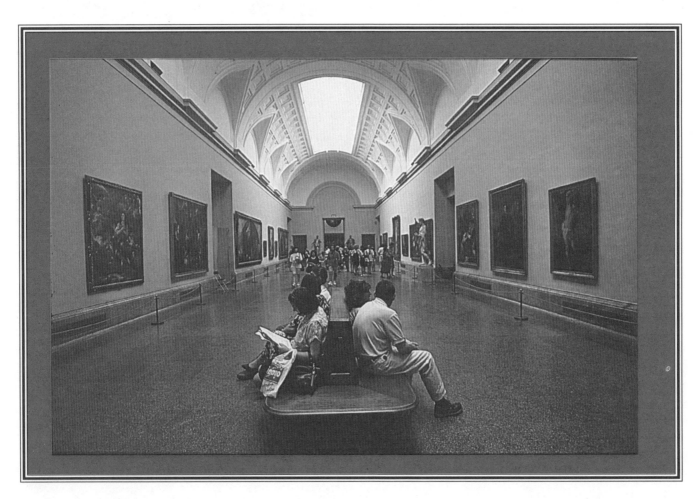

The Prado Museum
in Madrid

Your museum

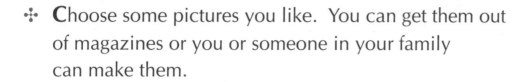

‡ **C**hoose some pictures you like. You can get them out of magazines or you or someone in your family can make them.

‡ **C**ut them out and paste them in the frames on this page. Start building up your own museum.

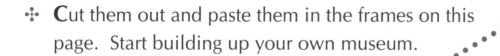

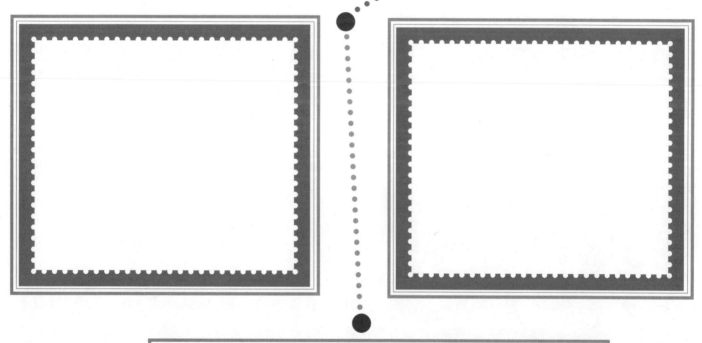

Bas-relief

✤ **S**culptures that show the outline of raised figures carved on a stone, clay, or wood surface are called bas-relief.

This form of art was very common in pre-Hispanic cultures. Bas-relief figures were painted with bright colors, that is, polychrome.

✤ **C**olor in this illustration so that it will look like a bas-relief.

✤ **Y**ou can highlight jewelry or clothing by adding bright colors.

Clay figure found on Jaina Island near Campeche, Mexico.

Sculpture

✧ **S**culpture is an art form in which many materials can be used: wood, iron, stone…

There are sculptures of many sizes. The biggest ones are in town squares, on streets, and in museums. Smaller ones can be found in homes, perhaps on top of a piece of furniture.

Sculptures are made by hand.
Each one is very special.

✧ **L**ook at these figures made by Peruvian artists.
What do you think they represent?

Handicrafts

✛ Jewelry is another artistic expression. One needs skill to know how to combine colors and materials to give form to necklaces, earrings, and bracelets.

Jewelry has always been a decorative object for men as well as women.

The most precious jewelry is made from gold or silver with precious stones.

Jewelry in other metals can also be made by hand by artisans.

✛ Can you make a necklace? Try it; it is very easy.

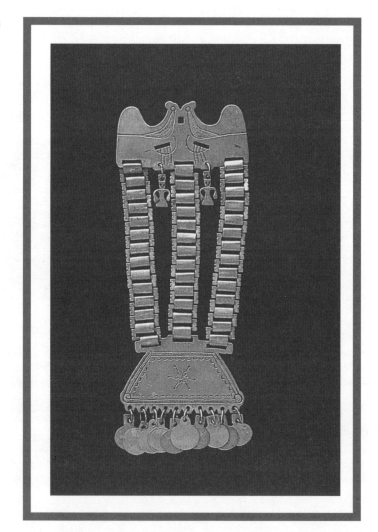

Silver piece made by Mapuche artisans in Chile.

Architecture

✤ Architecture is a science and an art at the same time.

Look at all these buildings built throughout history in different parts of the Hispanic world.

Look at the size, the decoration, the shapes of the columns, the roofs, and the towers.

Theater in Mérida, Spain.

Cathedral of Seville, Spain.

Pyramids of Monte Albán, Mexico.

Pyramid of Teotihuacán, Mexico.

✤ **Your turn.** Find a photo of any building you like and paste it on a piece of paper. Begin creating your own collection of architecture.

✜ David Díaz ✜

David Díaz's illustrations show a very personal and different way of using color, form, and space.

Sometimes David uses different materials for his compositions.

When there is a mixture of materials in a piece, we call it a *collage*.

David sometimes creates collages as backdrops for his paintings and then he draws over them.

David Díaz is a painter who has received many awards, among them the most important one in the United States given to children's book illustrators, the Caldecott Medal.

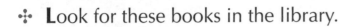

Your turn

✛ **L**ook for these books in the library.

✛ **D**o a drawing in a style like David Díaz's.

✛ **F**irst, create a collage and then paste your drawing on top of it.

✤ **O**ne of the easiest ways to create an illustration is by using pieces of paper.

All you need is sheets of colored construction paper or even newspapers. Tear them carefully by hand until they have the shapes that you want.

I spy

✛ **I**n this photograph, there are several handcrafted pieces.

✛ **D**o an inventory of what you see. (An inventory is when you make a list of everything there is in a place).

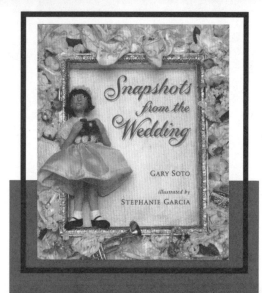

‡ Stephanie García ‡

In book illustration, many different materials can be used to create a picture.

It can be done with frames, cloth, sand, paint, or with clay figurines like the ones Stephanie García creates and dresses herself.

These photos of her creations are illustrations from the book *Snapshots from the Wedding*, written by Gary Soto.

Look closely at these illustrations.

Then the mariachis begin,
Trumpet blaring, the *guitarrón* thumping a beat,
The violins squeaking like mice,
The guitar singing like a bird cupped in your hands.

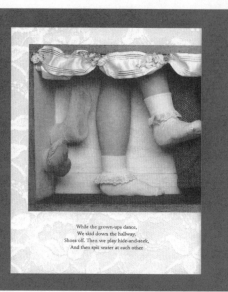

While the grown-ups dance,
We skid down the hallway,
Shoes off. Then we play hide-and-seek,
And then we spit water at each other

✦ **T**he book *Snapshots from the Wedding* is a story told in little vignettes.

✦ **Y**ou can also create a story about a party or celebration that you have experienced with your family.

✦ **D**raw the story in these four frames.

Origami

❖ **W**ith paper and a little patience, you can create amusing objects.

The art of creating little figures by folding paper into the shape you want is called origami.

Do you know how to make a hat from a sheet of newspaper?
Or can you make a paper boat that floats on the sea?

Ask anyone in your family to help you create objects out of a newspaper. Look at the penguin from both sides to inspire you.

❖ **W**rite a little story about your paper creation.

Textures

With colored tissue paper you can create patterns to serve as the background for an illustration.

- ❖ Take three or four pieces of tissue paper in different colors.
- ❖ Crumple them up.
- ❖ Flatten them out again and paste one of them to a piece of cardboard.
- ❖ Cut strips from the other three pieces.
- ❖ Paste them over the first piece.
- ❖ With wax crayons, color on top of the wrinkled surface.

Look what a wonderful effect!

✛ **C**loth has always been a material used to create beautiful pieces of art.

Cloth that has figures woven into it is called *tapestry*.

✛ **T**apestries are hung on walls like paintings. The Zapotec people of Oaxaca are great tapestry artists.

✛ **T**he *mola* is another form of making art with cloth. The mola is an artistic form from Panama in Central America.

✛ **E**mbroidery on dresses, shawls, tablecloths, or quilts also produces works of art.

Zapotec tapestry
in Mexico

Mola from Panama

✣ Beatriz Vidal ✣

Beatriz Vidal was born in Córdoba, Argentina, and now divides her time among that country, New York, and Paris. She creates paintings and illustrations.

She has also made drawings for television.

Her art is attractive and her drawings are very detailed. She is skilled in using color and painting animals.

These are some of the books illustrated by Beatriz Vidal.

Notice the care and respect she puts into painting diverse cultures.

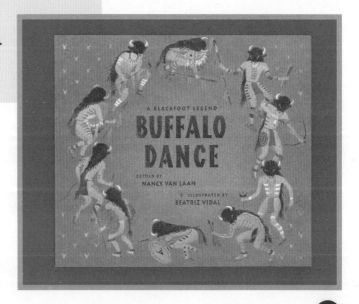

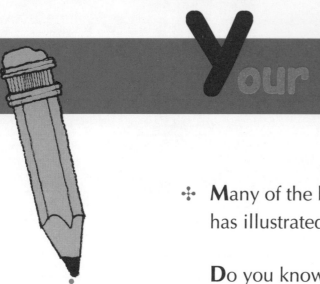

✣ **M**any of the books that Beatriz Vidal has illustrated are about legends.

Do you know any legends**?**

✣ **I**f you do, write one here. If you don't, look in the library for books on legends by Beatriz Vidal or by any other author and write a brief report on a legend here.

I spy

✣ **L**ook for a photo or illustration
that has many objects.

✣ **P**aste it to the blank space below, then
invite a friend to look for words that start
with the letter of one of the objects depicted.

I have learned to see

In this journal, we have shown you the many forms that art takes: toys, houses, cloth, jewelry.

Make a list of artistic creations you have seen and liked.

✤ In books _____

_____

✤ At school _____

_____

✤ In your city _____

_____

✤ In any other place you have visited _____

_____

I finished this journal

on _____.

I am _ _ _ _ _ _ _ years old.

I am a great artist,
because I learned to look.
I look at objetcs, buildings, and
clothes; nothing is exactly the same.
I want my world to be
beautiful and original.

❖ I have painted several paintings. Their titles are:

_____

_____

ACKNOWLEDGEMENTS

Page 5 / Diego Rivera, *Dream of a Sunday Afternoon in the Alameda*, detail, 1947-48. Museo de la Alameda, Mexico City. Copyright © 2000 Reproduction authorized by the Instituto Nacional de Bellas Artes y Literatura and Banco de México, Fiduciario en el Fideicomiso relativo a los Museos Diego Rivera y Frida Kahlo.

Page 6 / Francisco Jiménez and Simón Silva (illustrator), *La mariposa* (*The Butterfly*). Houghton Mifflin Company, Boston, 1998. Reprinted by permission of the publisher.

Page 6 / Alma Flor Ada and Simón Silva (illustrator), *Gathering the Sun/Juntar el sol*. Lothrop, Lee & Shepard Books, New York, 1997. Permission to reprint this cover is pending.

Page 8 / Frida Kahlo, *Self-Portrait,* 1930. Dolores Olmedo Collection. Copyright © 2000 Reproduction authorized by the Instituto Nacional de Bellas Artes y Literatura and Banco de México, Fiduciario en el Fideicomiso relativo a los Museos Diego Rivera y Frida Kahlo.

Page 8 / Francisco de Goya, *Self-Portrait.* Copyright © Museo del Prado, Madrid, Spain / Oronoz.

Page 10 / Ceramics workshop, Albacete, Spain. Photo by F. Ontañon, courtesy of the Tourist Office of Spain in Los Angeles.

Page 11 / Jeannine Atkins and Héctor Viveros Lee (illustrator), *Get Set! Swim!,* Lee & Low Books, Inc., New York, 1998. Reprinted by permission of the publisher.

Page 11 / Héctor Viveros Lee, *I Had a Hippopotamus*. Lee & Low Books, Inc., New York, 1996. Reprinted by permission of the publisher.

Page 12 / Interior of the Prado Museum, Madrid, Spain. Copyright © Walter Bibikow / The Viesti Collection, Inc., Durango, Colorado.

Page 14 / Drawing based on a clay figure from the island of Jaina near Campeche, Mexico. Museo Nacional de Antropología, Mexico City. From *Maya Design Coloring Book*, by Wilson G. Turner. Copyright © 1980 Dover Publications, Inc., New York.

Page 15 / Figures from Peru. Copyright © 2000 Santillana USA Publishing Company Inc. Photo by Lou Dematteis.

Page 16 / Silver jewelry made by Mapuche artisans from Chile. Copyright © Daniel Rivademar / Odyssey / Chicago.

Page 17 Cathedral of Seville, Spain. Copyright © Joe Viesti / The Viesti Collection, Inc., Durango, Colorado.

Page 17 / Theater in Mérida, Spain. Copyright © Joe Viesti / The Viesti Collection, Inc., Durango, Colorado.

Page 17 / Pyramid of Teotihuacán, Mexico. Copyright © 1994 Carl Rosenstein / The Viesti Collection, Inc., Durango, Colorado.

Page 17 / Pyramids of Monte Albán, Oaxaca, Mexico. Copyright © Marco / Ask Images / The Viesti Collection, Inc., Durango, Colorado.

Page 18 / Eve Bunting and David Díaz (illustrator), *Smoky Night*. Voyager Books, Harcourt Brace & Company, San Diego, 1999. Permission to reprint this cover is pending.

Page 18 / Eve Bunting and David Díaz (illustrator), *Going Home*. Joanna Cotler Books, HarperCollins Publishers, New York, 1996. Permission to reprint this cover is pending.

Page 22 / Cover and interior pages from *Snapshots from the Wedding* by Gary Soto, illustrated by Stephanie García, copyright © 1997 by Stephanie García. Used by permission of G.P. Putnam's Sons, a division of Penguin Putnam Inc., New York.

Page 26 / Zapotec Indian weaver, Oaxaca, Mexico. Copyright © 2000 Robert Frerck / Odyssey / Chicago.

Page 26 / *Mola* from Panama. Copyright © Joe Viesti / The Viesti Collection, Inc., Durango, Colorado.

Page 27 / Nancy Van Laan and Beatriz Vidal (illustrator), *The Legend of El Dorado: A Latin American Tale*. Alfred A. Knopf, Inc., New York, 1991. Permission to reprint this cover is pending.

Page 27 / Nancy Van Laan and Beatriz Vidal (illustrator), *Buffalo Dance: A Blackfoot Legend*. Little, Brown and Company, Inc., Boston, 1993. Reprinted by permission of the illustrator.